TRANSMATIC

BY CHRIS KELSO

"As a part-time hitman/ exterminator, Ignius
Ellis's dream is to buy a candy-apple red Nova
Supreme. In the process of trying to earn enough
cash to make his dream come true he gets sucked
into the rough world of Visitacion Valley, SF.
When the tenants in his apartment complex
reveal their various extracurricular activities,
this take an even more bizarre twist and Ellis
soon becomes acquainted with the nightmarish
Slave State dimension..."

For Darren Rae & Rachel Dickie
(Thanks for all the support)

TRANSMATIC   SS   CHRIS KELSO

MorbidbookS Is A Grotesque Bizarro Ballet Where The Most Profane Things Occur. An Impious And Perverse Dwelling Of Dark Revulsion. A Cozy Cottage Where Torture Porn And Brutal Bible Tales Are Devised. A Quiet Place To Relax And Spin Tales Of Depravity And Wickedness. A Halfway House For The Disturbed Where Rules No Longer Apply. A Safe Haven For Deviant Serial Killers To Hatch Their Wretched Schemes. Bring Your Pets.
The Tasty Ones Are Always Welcome.

https://www.morbidbooks.wordpress.com

TRANSMATIC SS CHRIS KELSO

ACCLAIM –

'Chris Kelso is a writer of almost intimidating intelligence, wit, and imagination. On every page, there is evidence of a great mind at work. Just when you're wondering if there are still writers out there who still feel and live their ideas out on the page, I come across a writer like Kelso, and suddenly the future feels a lot more optimistic. One calls to mind Burroughs, and Trocchi's more verbose offerings – whilst remaining uniquely himself, in a writer as young as he is, is a very encouraging sign, one of maturity that belies his youth. I look forward to reading more from him in the near future.'
– Andrew Raymond Drennan, author of The Immaculate Heart

"Chris Kelso sets his photonic crystal gun on KILL and takes no prisoners. My favourite era of science fiction was the 60s "New Wave" when the British magazine NEW WORLDS took front and centre, and there's a bit of NEW WORLDS here, kind of like Jerry Cornelius using the cut-up method in a bungalow in Glasgow, with a splash of Warren Ellis added for extra flavour. Kelso has a compelling voice. Somewhere Papa Burroughs is smiling."
–L.L. Soares, author of LIFE RAGE and IN SICKNESS

– 'Chris Kelso is an important satirist, I think it's safe to say.'
– Anna Tambour, author of Crandolin

– 'Come into the dusty deserted publishing house where mummified editors sit over moth-eaten manuscripts of books that were never written....anyone who enjoys the work of my late friend William Burroughs will feel welcome here with Chris Kelso.'   **– Graham Masterton**

- 'Chris Kelso's prose swaggers like blues and jitters like bebop. Dig.' - **Nate Southard, author of Down and Just Like Hell.**

- 'Sparky, modern, avant-garde but accessible, Chris Kelso's book is reminiscent of the most successful literary experimentation of the 60s and 70s, the sort of work that was published in the later New Worlds, but it's also thoroughly contemporary, intimately engaged with modern life as it is right now. Kelso steams with talent and dark wit and his blend of anarchy with precision is refreshing, inspiring and utterly entertaining . . .'
- **Rhys Hughes, author of Mister Gum**

- 'This emerging journeyman of the macabre has wormed his way into my grey-matter and continues to seep noxious ichor. I feel like I must devour him. Every little bit of him.'
- **Adam Lowe**

"Chris Kelso's writing is like a punch to the gut that forces your face against the page. The way his gritty prose carries his imagination is like a bar fight between Bradbury and Bukowski, with the reader coming out on top. The worlds he drags us into are so damn ugly that you have to admire their beauty."
- **Chris Boyle of BizarroCast**

- 'Whether he's writing about a fictionalized William Burroughs, Time Detectives, or Aliens Chris Kelso aims at the interstices or the Interzones because he understands that these are the people and spaces that define modern life – Kelso is also always funny and twisted.' - **Douglas Lain**

- *'Choke down a handful of magic mushrooms and hop inside a rocket ship trip to futuristic settings filled with pop culture, strange creatures and all manner of sexual deviance. '*
- Richard Thomas, author of Transubstantiate

- *'Guaranteed to uplift the heart of today's most discerningly jaded nihilist.'*   **- Tom Bradley**

- *'Chris Kelso is the one your mother warned you about. He is a sick, sick man - bereft of cure and heaped with symptom. His words will taint you irrevocably. Your eyes will want to gargle after reading just one of his stories.'*

- Steve Vernon, author of Nothing To Lose

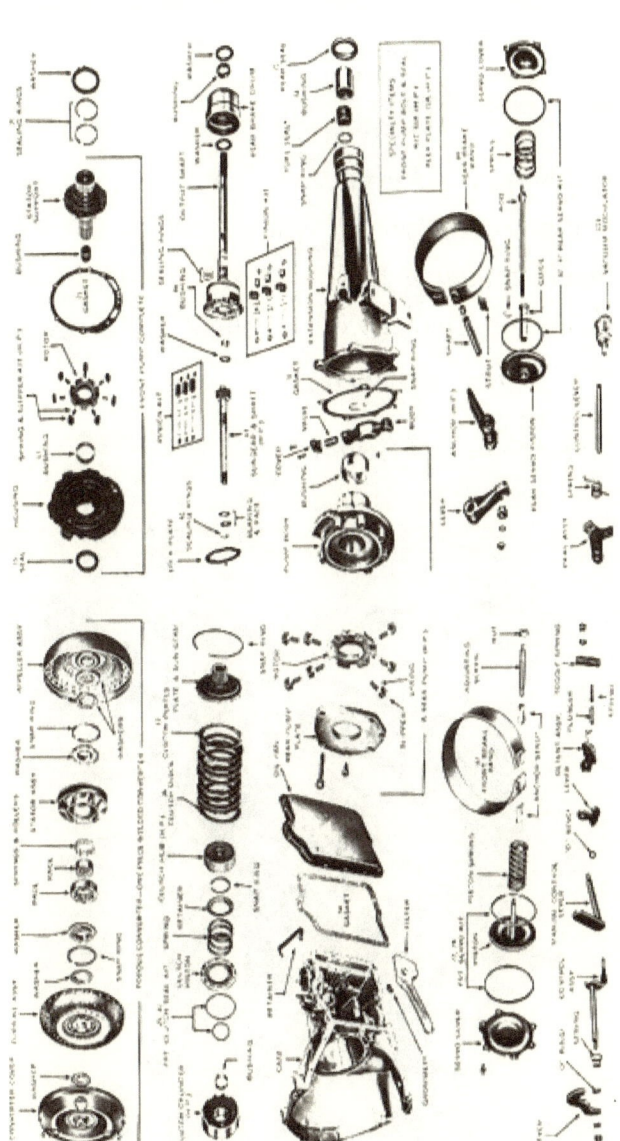

These days it takes all your energy just to get by in the present tense.

- You poor old man, that poor old man – says the gossiping wind. When every person is finally forgotten there will still be the heavy sediments of what we left behind in the streets of hell and in its gutters.

The architect's signature...

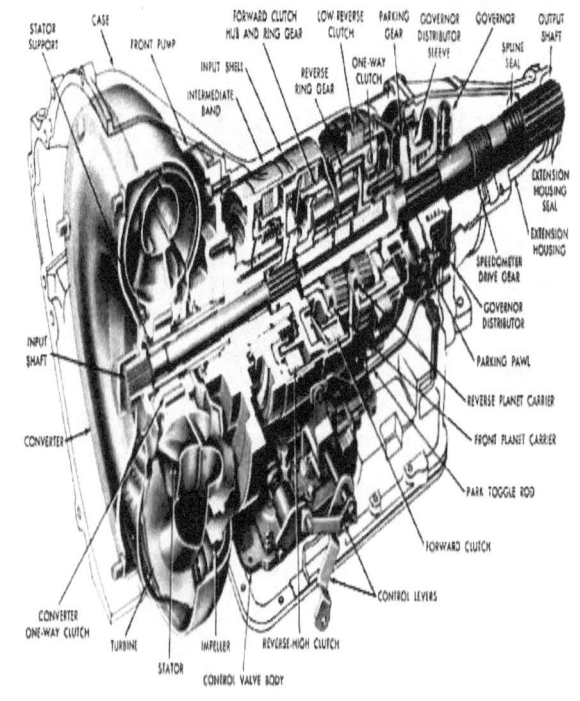

PART ONE

ONE

Ellis & Sur

IGNIUS ELLIS WAS A NUISANCE – most people in the East Quadrant certainly thought he was a nuisance. He had come to Visitacion Valley, San Francisco, to get away from Scotland, where *(of course)* everyone thought him a frightful nuisance.

– What about her? – Ellis asked, eying a gawky brunette bent over with a bag ready to pick up a dog shit, her buttocks about to burst out from between the tight fabric of a sarong. Sur craned his neck to the 5o'clock position to see who he was talking about.

– Who? Marie Sadlowidz? Shit man, she's a plucked chicken! Married for ten fuckin years…

– Bummer.

– Yeah, bummer.

– Hey, *she's* cute…

Sur craned to 9 0'clock.

– Yeah, she's a shape in a drape alright.

– What about her?

Sur craned to 2 o'clock.

– Henrietta Twaddle, varicose alley chick, handsome bitch but best to steer clear.

– What about her?

Sur went to crane to 6.30 but stopped at 5 o'clock.

– Hey, we ain't quail huntin' here, you crazy creep!

Ellis kept looking out the window. He was bored.

- This weather's a bastard eh?

- Would you give it a rest??

- I'm just gassing with ye mate!

- Shit man, you're so square you're practically a circle.

They watched their hit travel into a café called the RED ONION.

- He looks like a fuckin nutter – Ellis opined.

- Never mind if he looks like a fuckin nutter or not hepcat, just focus your attention on blowin his fuckin brains out and quite currin' like a damn barn-owl!

- I know…and I will focus…. but look at the state of his hair, look, he's got one of those cornrose hairstyles like a dodgy soul singer or somethin!

- Yeah, I see it, I see it…

- Look at his fuckin mental facial hair!

Sur turned in his seat to make serious eye contact with Ellis.

- Listen, you're new, so maybe you're not completely familiar with the house rules, but this is focus time ok? Just dummy-up, ya dig? Time to wise-up and do the job you're being paid to do, ok?

- Ok...I'm just sayin, it'll be a kick wasting this mental looking cunt.

- Focus your audio...

Sur was around 30 stone, a psychopathic eater, and had a flulike malaise about him always which Ellis later found out to be syphilis. He spoke like a hippie but didn't subscribe, Ellis noted that Sur had the ozone stink of a schizophrenic.

- What's he like, our hit?

- A little off the cob, but generally he knows his groceries.

- Why are we killing him again?

- Beats me man.

- He looks built.

- Built? He's built and everything plus! We gotta stay stealthy or we'll get our asses handed to us.

- So, when do we make a move?

- Shit man, there's plenty of time, ya dig?

- Sure, sure...

Ellis noticed other things about his partner - that his face seemed crushed by the mute hunger of lust, that he looked straight from the tallest dung heap in hell...

He was also a hired hit man and a deadly sonofabitch. Sur burst into life.

- Ok, let's go, remember, keep your head above the Mason Dixie Line.

- Sure...

Sur and Ellis rushed out either side of the car and headed towards the RED ONION. Ellis had no qualms with what this job entailed, but he couldn't help notice that the hit was *really* built – his shoulders were hunched with muscle and his neck was a pillar about 10 inches thick. Sur went into the RED ONION and signalled to Ellis to stay where he was. After a few minutes, there was commotion coming from the café and then the crack of a gunshot sent a flock of birds nesting on the roof of the building high into the firmament. People began flooding out of the Red Onion, including the heavy-built hit. Without thinking twice Ellis ran back to Sur's car and started up the engine setting off after him.

Dave Brubeck was on the radio….

He finally caught up to the hit who was bolting past the pharmacy in San Pablo. Ellis mounted the pavement and put his foot down on the accelerator until the hit's heels were scuffing the licence plate. For a moment, Ellis was worried that ploughing him down might damage the front of Sur's old lead sled. There wasn't enough time to worry about stuff like that though, he had to be bold. Mailboxes exploded and rectangular envelopes scattered over the streets in a ticker-tape-parade. Ellis crunched the ball of his heel into the accelerator and watched as the muscle-bound hit disappeared under the bonnet. A hyphen of blood spattered against the windshield. Ellis smiled victoriously. There were two subsequent bumps where both left-hand side wheels went over the body - his smile began a Cheshire grin. It *was* like hitting a deer. Ellis drove to the bottom of Paris Avenue and pulled over. He got out, looked down the street and saw a busted fire-hydrant sending a geyser of water into the air. The trail of destruction was immensely satisfying. He looked at the bloody bundle lumped in the middle of the road – the hit was dead. Sur appeared on the hill puffing and panting. People were looking on gawk-eyed but no-one had the guts to call the cops or reprimand Ellis for murdering the hit.

He enjoyed having that kind of power over people.

TWO

JUST BEFORE THE PLANET UNSTUCK from its Velcro and all the animals screamed and howled in confused despair, Ignius Ellis watched himself gasp at the future memory of dying in the mirror – unshakable shame passing through him in a final, fatal sweep all the while his head rests limp on its axle...

- I heard there's a re-development project going through congress to turn the 20 acres of this neighbourhood, including this apartment complex, into retail space. D'you think there's truth in that Mr landlord?

The landlord fidgeted and absent-mindedly cupped his left breast beneath his dressing gown.

- Mr Ellis, this part of town is a cesspit. The air *stinks* of metal, the rape gangs are out terrorising the streets EVERY-SINGLE-NIGHT, and there's no work for an honest American within 200 miles of Visitacion Valley. Do you really think it matters what they do with this place? It'll be piling shit on top of shit, stepping on one turd to replace it with another…

- I quite like it…

- And what do you *do* Mr Ellis? – The old landlord asked between intermittent strokes of his mangy cat's hide. His hardstone face grimaced.

- I'm in pesticide.

- Ah, an exterminator?

- Yes, well, no, mainly pesticides, *not* insecticides…

The landlord looked puzzled. Ellis brought out his card and handed it to the old man who instantly put it in the pocket of his dressing gown. His eyes glinted like agate.

- There's a difference – Ellis guaranteed.

- Yes, well, we have a small silverfish infestation in the building. If you could look I'd be most grateful.

Ellis gave a pained expression.

- Ach, see I'd love to, LOVE to, but that really falls under insecticide work. I don't deal with beasties, just rats and cats and, well, that's about it really. Maybe the occasional tiny spider in a bathtub....

- I see, well in that case rent is half a yard a week. No women, no animals, no backseat bingo with any cheap tricks, ya dig?

- Sure, and thanks again. I'm a bit of a chatterbox but I won't cause any harm, you have my word on that.

- Don't let the valley murder you Mr Ellis.

Ellis took the key from the old man and stuck it into the lock of apartment 4.11. He heard the chain from next door undo. A young African American stuck his head round into the hall.

- You the new tenant?

- I sure am — Ellis forwarded his hand for a shake. The neighbour met him halfway and came out into the corridor.

- I'm Mike Ryko.

- Ignius Ellis, pleasure...

- Say, that's a funky accent man, you Irish?

- Scots, I'm amazed someone understands me!

- Scots, well she-i-i-t, that's as good as Irish huh?

- I suppose so...

- Man, I love those Irish.

Ellis smiled, unsure what to say next.

- So, have you been in this building long Mike?

- Oh yeah. I inherited it from my grandma; she passed away 2 years ago. Sweet digs, if you don't mind old fussy drawers Layman. That nigger drinks blood and shits money.

- The landlord? Aye, I met him.

– That cat is Dixie fried!

– Dixie Fried?

– He's on so many meds for old age ailments he ain't really with it.

Ellis hadn't seen the inside of his apartment since the removal guys cleared out the old tenant's furniture. He tried to seem keen on Ryko's efforts at conversation.

– Don't forget little La across the hall. You *gotta* meet her.

Ellis looked to the door that ran parallel with his own.

– Who's La?

– A sweet little thing, total addict though. She lives there alone as far as I can tell. Don't know how she pays the rent.

– Is she a prozzie?

– Don't think so. She's taking part in this revolutionary new technique of rehab, but it's just an old fascist model on therapy. See, they break down her personality until she's totally dependent on her support officer, then they build and culture a new personality for her which won't get lost to drugs. Poor girl is a ghost, but she's real sweet...

- I'll keep an eye out....

- Then there's Mrs Kowalski. She lives in a timber shack on the roof.

- Is that allowed?

- Seems to be. Layman kind of leaves her alone, lets her use the washroom and the laundry-room whenever she wants. I've always thought that was kind of strange. We all live in big rectangular blocks forged from steel panels, you know, asbestos provides the building with its structural integrity and shit - but she lives in this separate construct made of plywood and old road-signs. She's got some son who's a rich jeweller, maybe that has something to do with it?

- Well, it's been good meeting you Mike.

SS

THE VERTICAL CONAPT APARTMENTS reached to the sky like stretched out angels falling into the swirling vortex of hell. Better to be in heaven or hell than stuck in between.

La was in Ellis's flat. He only met her that morning. She seemed to have been irrevocably traumatised by drug abuse, or maybe it was the therapy. La was a small-boned girl, no more than 17, with hair the colour of sun-burnt brick. Ellis thought she was an innocent enough looking kid who probably still thought women gave birth through their naval.

- Care for a drink? – Ellis asked her. She looked fragile and tiny sitting on his carpet-less floor.

- I'm allergic to alcohol.

- Ah, ok, no problem.

- Unless…unless you pour me a drink…if you pour me a drink, I'll drink it.

- Ok, but aren't you allergic?

- Yes.

- Well, what kind of reaction will you have to drinking it?

- I don't know. But if you pour me some wine I will drink it.

Ellis put some wine in a tumbler and forwarded it to her. *We're all on our way out tonight one way or another,* he told himself. She held the tumbler between her legs, cupped in her hands, without touching a drop. La seemed burdened by an indentured servitude, Ellis found this arousing but was instantly ashamed of those feelings.

- Do you want some of this? – He asked while fixing up a Jam Cap. She didn't look at all sure.

- If you fill the syringe up with it and stick it in my arm, I'll take it.

- Well, I…

The girl lifted her dress.

- Jab me with it if you like.

Ellis really wanted to be able to connect with La, but contemporary drugs could have an irreversible effect on a person's psyche. Everyone wanted to fuck and fight before the lights went out, this was never Ellis's style, despite what people thought. La left and went across the hall to a guy called Brady.

She'd get what she was after from him.

THREE

THE PHONE RANG.

- We got another job for you – emerged a voice distorted by a fazer-effect.

- Ok, great.

- You did good with the last hit, Sur says he'd work with you again, says you're spunky.

- Awe, that ol' softy…

- This Tuesday, free your schedule.

- Ah…

- What?

- That might be tough to swing.

- Excuse me?

- It's just, I have this job up at Arleta station, and it's kind of a contract I can't afford to break. If I do break it, they'll blacklist me and I won't work in the exterminator business again.

- You entered a binding contract with us, too.

- On the understanding, you'd give me at least a week's notice.

- Bullshit!

- You people don't pay me enough to jack in my other job, if you did I'd be more focused and enthusiastic.

- We can find another contract.

- Sur told me that's not the case.

- *Excuse me?*

- He said temp contracts are hard to sell. Killing people comes at a great cost to the hit and the hitman.

- EXCUSE ME??

- I need the money and you need a nutter who'll work part-time. You can change the day from Tuesday to Thursday, can't you?

- Thursday, clear your schedule.

- You got it.

There was a knock on the door. Ellis answered and was met with a middle-aged man with well quaffed hair and a zig-zag sweater.

- Are you the exterminator?

- Yes…

- My name is Brian Sector. I was wondering if you could help me kill a dirty rat in my bathroom.

- I'm not really on duty Brian.

- I'll pay you for it.

Ellis followed Sector across the hall to his apartment. He could hear La getting violently fucked through the spackle. Inside, Sector's place was a chaotic mess, like he'd been looted by a cack-handed burglar. Ellis picked up a large A2 sheet of paper with complex diagrams scrawled all over it.

– What's this?

– It's my plan for a Dyson Sphere...

– A what?

– An artificial megastructure encompassing a star that can extrapolate energy.

– I see...

– Sorry about the mess – he said moving a mass of books from the couch to create a place for Ellis to sit. He opted to stand instead.

– It's a palace compared to my flat. Bet old Layman loves coming to collect his rent from you, nah I'm kidding of course. A palace this is, an absolute palace. So, what do you do Mr Sector?

- I'm a physician actually – he revealed after a moment's hesitation.

- Ah right, did you treat young La?

- I tried, for a while…

- She's pretty banged up, eh?

- I thought for a while that I could help her. I don't at all approve of the Fascist therapy she's being subjected to.

- You thought you could *help* La? You must be a confident shrink?

- Only the wounded physician can hope to heal.

Ellis smiled and decided he quite liked Brian Sector.

- So, shall I look at this filthy rat of yours?

- I've changed my mind about that. Let it be.

- Ok, fair enough. That's one lucky rat!

- Tell me, do you know about the Eye?

- Emm…no I can't say that I do – Ellis perched on the armrest of a couch. The fabric had been blanched by spilt liquid but it was surely cleaner than anywhere else in the apartment.

- The Eye is what helps you see.

- Self-explanatory I suppose.

- There is a state of being that you must go through. You should be willing to undergo a painful transformation. A state called Transmatica.

- Sounds easy.

- Nothing could be harder. You must be one of the select few who are transmatic. If you're not, well…the less said about it the better.

- No tell me!

Ellis wriggled his buttocks on the arm-rest getting comfy, his intrigue piqued. Sector leaned forward as if worried that the wrong person might overhear.

- Well, there was a fellow who lived in this building, not far from your own apartment who wanted to experience The Eye. He was so sure he was transmatic.

- What happened?

- His head exploded.

- Oh…

- And then his arms fell off…

- Oh…

- And then his legs fell apart at the knees.

- Oh?

- And then his genitals ruptured and his anus prolapsed.

- Ok, I think I'm about sold on this product. Thanks anyway Mr Sector.

Ellis stood up and made towards the door, ready to say his farewells, when Sector stood up and gave an apologetic expression with his mouth and eyes.

- Please it is a little shocking…

Ellis found it curious why Mike Ryko hadn't mentioned Sector in the hallway before.

- You should be willing to give up the Solipsis, that's why it didn't work for him….

- And what's Solipsis?

- The internal mind and its relationship with the external body. It's an attachment that only leads to agony. I can tell you are in a state of all-engulfing Solipsis…

- I don't have enough time for all this Mr Sector, but listen, thanks all the same…

- You don't have time? We all have time; it's a luxury of being alive.

- It's just I have more than one job ye see…

- And is one job not sufficient?

Ellis didn't like Sector's tone one bit.

- I'm saving up for enough money to buy a car if you must know.

- You can't afford a car on an exterminator's wage?

- It's a certain type of car, a candy apple red Nova Supreme.

- Sounds ostentatious.

- Well, I have other luxuries I like to indulge in too Mr Sector.

- Ah, drugs, material things, the trappings of a small mind...

Ellis had reached the apogee of his patience. Now Sector had taken to cheap digs, Ellis decided it was time to bring out the nasty just to show him who was really in charge here.

- I'm a hitman too actually doctor – he said as off-handedly as he could muster - It brings in the extra cash I need and satisfies my, er... *darker* urges, know what I mean?

Sector looked unfazed.

- Please leave...

Ellis obliged and left the door half open.

– Good luck with that rat – he hollered from the hall.

FOUR

Thursday

SOMEHOW THERE WAS ALWAYS the fresh fragrance of pruned wisteria in the air outside Mrs Kowalski's hut. The place was always flooding because it ran flush with the surface of the roof and rainwater from the gutter often seeped under the rot-wood porch. It had no indoor plumbing and the damp air of the place bred fatal coughs.

She never left the shack. Nothing went in and nothing ever went out – except maybe the dry breath of smoke puking out of a cast iron vent above the overhang bracket.

Ignius Ellis and Mike Ryko were standing about 100 meters from Mrs Kowalski's shack.

- We should see what really goes on in there, man – Ryko said while jamming a twisted nail into the sole of his boots.

- What're you doing?

- There's a riot before sun-down, can't hurt to be prepared man. So, do you want to?

- Do I want to what?

- Check out Kowalski's hut?

- No.

- Well, why not?

- I don't want to mate, that's all.

- Why not?

- Dunno, just doesn't seem…right.

- As if that stuff matters *now*.

- It matters to me. I'm old fashioned mate. Leave the old bird be.

- Well I'm going to see what's going on.

- Well I better get ready for work.

- Oh yeah, the extermination industry waits for no man!

- You got it mate!

Ellis descended the roof staircase. He thought about Ryko for a moment. Ellis didn't like the thought of him snooping about some poor old biddy's house.

SS

SUR WAS WAITING IN THE LEAD-SLED out front. He seemed happy to see Ellis, the sight of Sur's big jolly face warmed Ellis too - reminded him of a Venus in a conch. His hair was long and scraped back into a tight shank, his forearms and neck were set in ropes of thick blue veins beneath the bunched-up sleeves of a stained peasant blouse. Sur always wore dingy vagrant hand-me-downs; on this occasion, he was wearing cotton corduroy trousers with sandals.

- Hey Grand Theft Auto, what's happnin' hepcat?

- Plodding along mate. You keeping well aye?

- Jesus man, you are nonstop! Ha-ha! Hey I respect your upbeat attitude. I'm well, and you're well too, huh?

- Aye, working hard. The folk in my building are a bit nutty mind you.

- If you think someone is nutty they must be a downright boneafide screwball!

- So where we goin? Who we wasting?

- We're goin to 45 Leland Avenue at Desmond Street. The sick creep we're gonna put to rest is a rotten little Jew, goes by the name Kowalski, that's all I know.

- Hey, hey, careful now.

- What?

- We're hitmen not anti-Semites!

Sur gave a big smile.

- California was *made* for cats like you Ignius.

He powered up the lead-sled and made off down McLaren Park. Ellis was watching the beautiful women glide by when some stark realisation hit him hard in the gut.

- Hey, what did you say his name was again?

- What, the hit? Kowalski?

- Shit…

- What is it?

- I have a neighbour in my building called Kowalski, some senile old coot.

- This dude is in his 30's man, he's just struck it big in the jewellery market.

- Ok…

- You gonna be ok to do the hit?

- Sure.

SS

IN TRUTH, ELLIS DIDN'T KNOW how he felt about all this. Back in Scotland he was considered something of a thug to some people – he never shied away from anything in his life. But there was something about Mrs Kowalski's situation that unsettled him, all alone up there in that shack. Most old people reminded Ellis of his own sweet grandma. If something ever happened to make her unhappy Ellis would kick up shit like you've never seen. It sickened him to think about his grandma in pain. He thought about the pain Mrs Kowalski would feel…

SS

THEY ARRIVED AT DESMOND STREET and Sur parked outside a fenced off toxic clean-up site. Night fell quickly and they saw the hit pull up before getting out of his car – a candy-apple red Nova.

– I'm saving up for that car you know?

– You are? That's swell. I bet Ray Romano over there bought that baby with his extra pennies he had just lying around.

Ellis appreciated what Sur was trying to do. He was trying to make him feel better about killing Mrs Kowalski's kid. The hit had hair growing from below his chin the way pine might grow tenaciously from a cliff edge.

- You want to pop him the old-fashioned way, or plough him down with my lead-sled again in front of a dozen witnesses?

Ellis sniggered and took the gat.

- What's he doin anyway?

- I have no idea…

Kowalski was trying to unload a bundle of something wrapped in bloody linen from the boot of his Nova.

- What the…?

The draped bundle thumped onto the sidewalk.

- Is that…a *body*? – Ellis couldn't believe what he was seeing.

- Sure, looks like it hepcat.

Kowalski dragged the stiff into the side entrance of a Launder-O-Mat called *CLEAN&SWIRL*.

– Let's go.

SS

SUR AND ELLIS GOT OUT of the car and moved towards the hit. Ellis felt something serious afoot, it made his stomach do flip-flops and he didn't like it. Sur inched his massive back across the brick wall of the CLEAN&SWIRL, gun poised, ready and raised at his chin. Ellis, crouching, followed behind. The sound of churning washing machines meant they could sneak in unheard, even a man of Sur's considerable size could walk around undetected. Ellis cocked his own weapon, he felt comfortable with hand-guns. He used to own one back when he was a football hooligan, it was his way of putting the fear of god into sheep-shagging away supporters - a .44. Sur made a gesture with his mouth to indicate that the hit was in the next room and he wasn't alone. They both crouched and peeked into the store-room.

Ellis had forgotten the specific event that had started his decline into entropy.

– I thought the hit was supposed to be alone?? – Ellis whispered.

Kowalski and a small Asian man were cutting the bloody rags apart from the corpse.

Ellis recognised the body straight away.

It was Mike Ryko.

SS

THE ASIAN MAN OBVIOUSLY OWNED the Launder-O-Mat. He had a uniform on with the CLEAN&SWIRL insignia on it, his name-badge read MANAGER.

– This is the sonofabitch who tried to rape my dear old momma.

The Asian man observed the corpse and looked forlorn.

– Poor Negro.

- Yeah, yeah, poor Negro. Help me get rid of this fuckin body.

- Ok, wait a moment.

Ellis couldn't believe what he was hearing – *would Ryko really try to rape Mrs Kowalski?* If he did, then Ellis couldn't honestly blame her son for killing him. He knew about the rape gangs that trolled the streets of Visitacion Valley. Often, they'd been groomed since sixth grade by vicious criminals, but Ryko seemed so well-intentioned. The Asian man returned with a carton of something.

- This is a very special mix.

- What is it?

- Acid mainly.

- Why do you need acid in here?

- In case any important investors need little problems taken care of…

SS

KOWALSKI AND THE ASIAN PROPRIETOR grabbed either end of Ryko's limp cadaver and carried him back out into the alley. Sur and Ellis tip-toed not far behind. They watched as Kowalski flipped the lid of a dumpster and helped squeeze Ryko into it, covering over his body over with heavy handfuls of trash. The Asian man tipped the canister of acid in after. A thick column of steam swelled out from beneath the lid and high into the night sky. The sounds of metal rusting and crunching as the acid tore its way through the dumpster's bowels went on for a good few minutes. When the acid trail stopped and silence returned Kowalski began addressing his partner in crime. In hushed tones.

- You know my mother told me to be careful of this guy.

- Mrs Kowalski told you that?

- Yes, she says Mr Ryko here had a gift.

- What kind of gift?

- Transmatica…

- You mean…the Negro was transmatic?

- Apparently. He seems like a self-absorbed sonofabitch too, I don't know how someone like that could silence the Solipsis?

- Typical, that a man who tries to rape an elderly woman is in possession of such a rare gift, typical…

Sur stood up and walked towards them casually, his gun stretched out in front of him.

- Ok scum-fucks…

Kowalski and the Asian didn't seem totally caught off guard. Sur popped a slug into the tiny Asian's forehead and he went down like a child who'd just been struck with a cement dodge-ball. Sur was about to ice the hit and complete the job when Ellis appeared from over his shoulder and took aim.

– He's mine…

Kowalski put two hands in the air and grinned.

- What ye grinning at mate? I'm about to fucking kill you!

- You really have no idea who you're dealing with do you?

- I know who you are.

- You'll see the Cycle coming if you look hard enough. The clouds will amass and the lights in the distance shut off in a domino effect before the streets lamps in your area go the same way. An awful growling wind arcs and pulls the peripheral environment apart until your left in dismantled chaos. Then the death-comas will start spreading and you'll all go under.

- Eh…?

- SHOOT HIM HEPCAT! – Sur screamed before raising his own gun and firing a round straight into Kowalski's throat. He fell, legs buckled, making a hideous choking sound.

- Do you think anyone would notice if I took his car?

PART TWO

FIVE

– I'VE MADE A CONSCIOUS EFFORT to enjoy each day before restoration – 15 minutes of calisthenics every day.

Dr Sector spoke away inattentively while setting up complex apparatus. A young student sat in a chair with a metal helmet lodged onto his skull that had various wires leading into a portable machine. The student appeared malnourished, as if a lack of oxygen had left him in a state of perpetual biodegradation. He wore grey drainpipes and had dull features – the features of an imbecile, small slow moving eyes and poor reactions. His mind seemed a dustbin of battling thoughts, all bad ones.

Ellis sat on the crap-cluttered couch and watched.

- The subliminal messages coming from this realm stimulate the Amygdala, tricking the brain into believing that the artificial world around them is real.

- So, are you able to switch off your Transmatica then?

- I'm not actually Transmatic, but I am dedicated to finding those who are in the faint hope that we can unlock the secret to freedom for humanity.

The young man in the chair didn't say a word. He looked completely focused. Sector strapped a Velcro cuff around his arm and the young man gave a faint smile to suggest he was ready.

- What's the *real* world like? – Ellis asked while nibbling the dowel of bone at his knuckle.

- We believe it to have some resemblance to this one. I think there's an element of pre-attentive processing, or unconscious information gathering from the real plane of existence. Our brains are picking up ghost memories of the lowest level of the 4rth dimension...

- Eugh...this is all a bit...well, daft, isn't it?

- If it's daft then you'll have no qualms about sitting in for processing after young Billy here?

- You'll be telling me to wipe my arse with three seashells next. I just came here to ask you about Mike Ryko doctor.

Sector's face suddenly bled of its colour.

- What do you know about Ryko?

- He was in the apartment next to mine.

- How typical that leech should try to influence you. He does this with all new tenants.

- I liked Mike...

- *You* would! He appeals to the working-class ethic of the lowest common denominator. That's his angle. False sense of security you see.

- I assume you knew he was Transmatic?

- Mike Ryko was *not* Transmatic Mr Ellis, he had powerful psionic abilities, but they were nothing to do with penetrating the subcutaneous jelly of the Solipsis. He could never get that far, he was too self-involved, like you...

- They're saying he tried to attack Mrs Kowalski on the roof, do you think that's true?

- It's true, I saw him...

- You did? And did he...you know..." rape" anyone?

- Ryko is an animal and that is his biggest barrier to true Transmatica. His lusts could not be suppressed.

Ellis smiled to himself. Billy who was hooked up to the strange apparatus looked deep in doubtful reflection, interviewing his own brain.

- Mrs Kowalski is a dear, sweet old woman. I would've killed him if I hadn't been a slave to my own fear. He was a brute...

- Well, Mike is dead.

Sector's expression seemed to betray his previous statement – he looked saddened by this news.

– It was only a matter of time.

– So, you're not surprised?

– Surprised? Hardly, the man had more enemies than I care to mention.

– I still say I liked Mike and I'm convinced that somehow, he's getting an unfair trial. What does Mrs Kowalski have to do with Transmatica?

Sector fell silent. There was a sense that too much had been revealed already.

– We really must push on with this auditing…

– Must be some gift…

– If you sit in for processing we can find out if you have it.

– I don't think so mate, not after the story about that cunt who's head and arse exploded!

- That was just to scare you. It's perfectly safe!

- D'you make a habit of fear mongering Dr Sector?

- Will you try it, or are you a slave to fear? I suspect you're probably terrified...

- If it'll shut you up! What's all that shite you're wiring the scruff up with?

- It's my processing equipment. We can tell if he's Transmatic or not. Stand back.

Sector flipped a switch and currents travelled through a series of tubes leading into Billy's forearms. Ellis took a step backwards. Sector explained

- The way Transmatica works is that, if you're lucky enough to possess the subconscious ability to process, then once you experience the real world you never forget it. You see in a sort of split screen, both universes simultaneously. Transmatic individuals begin to reject the poison being transmitted until eventually it's powerless on them...

– Poison shyness?

– Excuse me?

– Poison shyness. It's an inherited behaviour among animals in my trade…a rodent or feline learns not to fall for exterminator poison, it gets a taste for it. Often the rat smells the antimicrobial agent from a mile away and recoils from it.

– Transmatica is more than just a learned response.

– But it's similar.

– No, it's not. It's more like amnesia, where we recall past knowledge from the universe and humanity in general. Now stand back please.

Billy started thrashing around until he fell sideways, toppling his chair over onto the floor. Ellis looked anxious.

– It's a somatic experience this is supposed to happen.

Sector knelt to the quivering body and tried to control it.

- Follow the alluvium trail Billy!

Ellis looked unconvinced.

- He's having a seizure you mental cunt!

- He can see the imminence of the Cycle.

- Christ...

- Don't trust the moon! - Billy started yammering.

- Eh?

Dr Sector shushed Ellis. Billy went on.

- The moon is behind all of this!

- It is...?

- It manipulates our minds, tunes our consciousness to the wrong wavelength, the artificial one. The moon is a spacecraft broadcasting the fake world directly to the zonked-out left hemispheres of our brains.

- Your brain is pickled big man….

- Mr Ellis please! – Sector had manoeuvred Billy into the emergency position.

- I'm outta here I've a job to do.

SS

–RAT CATCHERS OF OLD CAPTURED vermin with trained dogs or with their bare hands, much less holistic. Things are a little different now. Catching and breeding rats used to be an affluent occupation. The risk of being bitten or catching a disease was worth decent money way back when…

Mr Layman was busy controlling his frantic wife who detested creepy crawlies. Ellis went on waving his industry standard B&G gallon sprayer around gesticulating his point.

- I used to be a garbage man at one point back in Scotland. I suppose I have this compulsion to take out the trash…

Ellis laughed out loud but no one was listening to him. He heard the scuttling of insect feet on linoleum and dropped to his knees to scan the area. Ellis saw a tapered abdomen disappear beneath the fridge. Layman's wife was hysterical with fear, cowered in the corner with her feet curled up to her chin.

- I think I've found the source of your infestation.

- My wife is terrified of bugs...

- Christ, get rid of them, god, my skin, they're on me somehow...my skin is crawling just looking at them...having them in my house is...oh god, just horrid, please, kill them. Step on them; kill their family, all of them...

- They mostly eat sugar, but can go after glue, book bindings, coffee, dandruff, you name it...

- Oooooohhh, kill 'em, kill 'em!

- They were one of the first animals to colonise dry land you know?

- Step on them, just step on them. You don't need that contraption, never mind all that kafuffle, just put your foo5t into their skulls!

- If you want to take your wife out of the kitchen and break a tranquiliser into her Pims that'd really help me out…

Layman escorted his wife into the living room while Ellis pulled the refrigerator away from the back wall. The huge nest of silverfish was bulging out of a hole in the plaster. Ellis flinched as he inspected the grey hue and metallic shine of the alien intruders, the female had just produced a gossamer covered sperm capsule.

- Eugh…see *this* is why I don't do insects!

Ellis took out his brass wand, pumped at his pack mule and took aim - a haze of chemical bacterium shot of the shaft and into the nest. Ellis could swear he heard their screams of agony. Freshly hatched nymphs, barely moulted, perished at his hand. Ellis drew satisfaction from the slaughter, he was the war pornographer. He waited for the poison fog to clear so he could inspect the results of the massacre, but it refused to disperse. Instead it grew thicker, until Ignius couldn't breathe...

SIX

ELLIS LIFTED HIS HEAD. La was standing there. He felt a harsh Martian wind on his bones and realised he was stark naked and cuffed to a cave wall. Outside there were the vague verticals of a ruined, reeking city. *This must be hell* – Ellis thought.

Still better than Visitacion Valley...

He felt blighted by fatigue and confusion. It was akin to taking a bad Jam Cap...

- I'm glad you're awake. We can get on with the procedure now.

- La? What are you doing, I...?

The girl seemed confident and womanly. Ellis had to do a double take to make sure it was her. She was wearing a strange reflective spacesuit, tight fitting and shimmering. She still had her ferocious sexuality, a need to be exploited.

– You little bitch!

– The Slave State doesn't answer to anyone. They simply take what they want without consequence. There is no higher power you can go off and complain to.

La skirted back and forth, left to right like a demented spider.

– Who *are* you, aside from a wily wee minx?

– I'm an official representative of the State, a hard-wired drone. In that respect, we're not so different. One day you may be sent a message instructing you to come and work in the mining enclaves, until that day you will roam the Slave State dimension and try and live the fractured life of a pathetic insect.

– That sounds ideal aye…

La loosened Ellis's shackles and he fell to the stone hard on his knees.

- What are you talking about? What's a fuckin Slave State? I'm no cunts slave!

- It doesn't matter. I don't *have* to explain, I was going to clear things up as a courtesy, a sort of thank you for being kind to me before when we both met in purgatory. But if you're going to be arrogant and aggressive then you can stick a fence pole up your asshole.

Ellis rubbed his wrists where the metal shackles had left raw rings.

- Was Mike in on all this?

La arched her back, pushing her ass out. Ellis could smell inhuman lust on her.

- No. Mike Ryko was indeed transmatic, you are not, despite what you've been led to believe. It was simply your time to come here. You had no influence over the decision. No one has *any* say in when they cross over to the true dimension, nor should they have. That's why Ryko was murdered. He was a threat to the balance of power. Anyone with Transmatic ability is a threat. We can't afford any Pax Romana here, chaos is integral to out survival.

- Kowalski is one of you??

- The Kowalski Immitant isn't even a real person, they're both a manifestation of people dreamed into existence by the State.

- This is preposterous darlin'

- I know this must all be very shocking for you.

- Well aye...

- One positive thing is that you can live some sort of life until you receive your message of conscription. Use the time wisely.

- What if I kill myself?

- Then you'll be dead...obviously.

- Oh...

- Your dimension exists as a kind of limbo, a between place. At our leisure, we pluck unwitting homunculi from the bottom tier. We did not create your realm, but we are in almost complete control of it and its content.

- What about Sur, was he in on this?

- No. He's just another hapless sap, but his time will come. You'll be re-united in the enclaves soon enough.

Ellis sensed she would perhaps still accept him sexually, even now. If she wanted to fuck like she did before it wouldn't be anything resembling human intimacy – it would be conducted in the fashion of orgying flies crawling over each other in the belly of a filthy stool pigeon, spread across a cradle of litter and debris; fucking without pleasure, without meaning, without anything but root desire. Although La looked so alluring in her tight, gleaming jumpsuit, the thought of sex with her now repulsed Ellis. La had a Silverfish stare, compound eyes. She seemed so pure and decent before. Ellis had a desire to exterminate her like a cockroach. He felt she may have wanted this too…

- You've learned a terrifying truth about the nature of the universe.

- What's that?

- That it doesn't have a soul. Like Plato suggested, the irrational streak running through the world's soul is in fact, a copulating insane machine. The Mind behind it all is an insane weirdo.

_SS_

HE CRAWLED FROM THE CAVE and down the stony face of the mountain towards Shell County. He was aware of his nakedness but wasn't inhibited by it. At the bottom, he looked up to see La looking down. He couldn't see the features on her face. The mask had slipped…

Outside parked on the curb was a candy apple red Nova…

SEVEN

THE SOLIPSIS, THE CYCLE, THE 4TH dimension - these were all just buzzwords in the intricate final deceit Ellis had existed in his whole life. He was angry about that. It occurred to Ellis that he could track down Mike in the Slave State. He must be here somewhere, unless the State had ordered him executed because of his power?

SS

- ***"HI THERE EVERYONE, THIS IS*** *Phil Dick, coming to you direct on KSMO radio station, Shell County to Moosejaw, Wire City to the Zinc Theatre, this is your number 1 source of music for lovers of classical and jazz. We've got some great numbers on the way, but first up is Art Tatum with "Body-And-Soul!"*

SS

ELLIS TURNED OFF THE RADIO. Even driving in his candy apple red Nova, he couldn't experience even the faintest stitch of happiness. He also missed Sur, a man he'd only met twice in his entire life. There was something tragic about that realisation too. Ellis coasted through the streets of Shell County, past the gin soaks, stew bums and warped veterans that lined the pavements; past the storefronts, windows smashed and contents looted – it was almost like Visitacion Valley, all it needed were a few rape gangs. It wouldn't take long adjusting to life here...

SS

IGNIUS PULLED OVER OUTSIDE A bar called THE WIFEBEATER. He thought he'd ask around to see if anyone knew of Mike. Inside the place looked and smelled like death. Ellis walked to the bar and saw a well-dressed man to his left.

– Hi pal...

The well-dressed man stirred as if he'd just woken up. He was by all accounts completely pissed.

– Eh, oh...I'm Pushkin. I'm an editor.

- I'm Ignius. Have you seen a fella called Mike Ryko?

- Christ, I don't know…

Pushkin put his head in his arms as if to go back to sleep. Ellis nudged him back to attention.

- He's about 5 foot 9, black, real sunny disposition?

- Sunny disposition?

- Aye...?

- If there's someone in Shell County with a sunny disposition then point them out so I can alert the proper authorities. Listen bub, ain't no one here got a sunny disposition, ok?

- I gathered as much.

- I hate to be the bearer of bad news too, but he might have already been taken to the enclaves or assassinated in broad daylight.

- Mike was my only friend in the world. Well, him and big Sur…

- Ain't it just the way? Since the holocaust, everyone wants to write their autobiography, can you believe that shit?

- What holocaust?

- Fuck me, you *are* new!

- Well sure.

- Everyone has their own perspective on the disaster and of the resulting outbreak which saw each man, woman and child in Shell County turned into a hideous reanimated monster. As an editor that's a dull way to make a living.

- I'm sure it's deeply unsatisfying. Have you seen my friend or not?

- No.

Ellis sat on the stool defeated. Pushkin hailed the barkeep.

- Get our new friend a drink.

- Cheers. I'll have whatever's on tap.

The barkeep came back with a jug of frothy beer. Ellis brought the pint to his lips and couldn't contain a whimper of pleasure.

- Fuckin horrible beer – he concluded - but it's the first one I've had in almost a decade.

- You gave up?

- I had to. I was killing everyone around me.

- I bet you just found out the world you lived in was a heap of dogshit?

Ellis nodded.

- So, what, the moon was an artificial satellite, it still looked beautiful, did it not?

- I suppose so.

- You know before you wake up in that cave and you're told about all the disinhibiting stimuli originating from Sirius and all that other irrelevant bull, the moon was the most peaceful, benign looking thing you'd ever seen...

- So, what *is* this place?

- It's hard to give it one single name. It's part Narcokleptocracy, because the drug runners of the solar system fund the whole thing; part Kerdocracy, because the ultimate rules are based on material gain; part Raubwirtschaft because they plundered our economy; part military junta...

- Ok, so it's a shite-hole.

- Oh yeah. If I had to give it a name, if I *had* to...I'd say it was an Obligorarchy, because the Lumpbourgiouse alien race that oversee it all are trying to amend the damage they initially caused. It was *their* radon gases that destroyed earth first time round. Then they took responsibility, said they'd do everything in their power to build it back up again. Well, they sure did, but the humans left are working as slaves where the unpaid work has no purchase power. Though, the Slave state blueprint existed before any colonisation occurred.

- I'm confused...

- Yup.

- I've had a bad Jam–Cap and I'm high…

- Ingroup favouritism and collective narcissism, it's part of their exegesis.

- I don't feel much like drinking anymore…

- Don't look so sad man. We're just DNA carriers capable of experience, we're no great loss. It's the publishing industry that gets me…

- Oh…?

- You see, the main problem is that all the stories are the same and since the fall of the publishing industry, there's no filter for the work being disseminated. Aside from the fact most of them can't write because their hands won't keep still and their fried minds are always preoccupied by the intrinsic hunger for brains.

Ellis took another draft of his beer. Pushkin was a bulky man with hair combed back with too much lacquer. He looked important, successful.

- Oi, I swear, if I read one more longwinded description of a fuckin' zombie eating a delectable human brain, I'll scream.

- Aye?

- I. WILL. FUCKING. SCREAM.

- Fair enough.

- Anyhoo, not to be a fickle Freddy, I made the most of this situation. Hey, what else could I do? I set up my business and put a sign that says **OPEN** outside the door. I watch the undead idiots pour in, fucking POUR in! I didn't say that what I do isn't lucrative, just dull.

- Everyone must make a dollar I suppose.

- For one reason or another I was not turned into a starving abomination by the Slave State virus - more bizarre even than that is the damn zombies won't touch me either (any cracks about my brain not being plentiful enough, well, just save it! I left my sense of humour back in Wire City with my ex-wife and her condo). This one slobbering moron comes to me and groans something about editing and publishing his piece-of-shit bio. He drops a sports bag full of crisp green notes onto my desk. He says it's mine, just clean up his manuscript and get him a publisher. He says this book just HAS to get out there. I ask him who he is and he grins a toothless, rotted grin. He says Baroness Un wants his book published by the best in the business. I was flattered and confused. You see, the baroness had died about a month before. I tell the zombie fuck-head this and he shuffles closer. He says that Un ain't dead at all, that he faked his death after an assassination attempt.

- Who's Un?

- Christ, that's too long to explain man, just try and keep up...

- Ok.

- Back when I owned Subterfuge I was a real highflyer.

- You've certainly got the threads Mr Pushkin.

- People wonder why I stay in Shell when I could get out there and work on some credible books.

- Well, why don't you?

Pushkin gave Ellis a look that suggested the answer was patently obvious.

- Oh aye, no-one can leave. Shit…

- I tell those people that the parched hills of Shell County are where the *real* work is. Artistic integrity means jack shit to me. I think baroness Un knew this.

SS

ELLIS STOOD UP FROM HIS stool and finished the last of his beer. He put one hand on Pushkin's shoulder and thanked him. Pushkin put his head back in his arms as if to go back to sleep.

EIGHT

HE WAS A CRAPULOUS OLD MAN, the doctor. He often drubbed neighbourhood children with his cane. The old man's hard-on poked out in the playground. His hair wasn't grey yet, nor was it the buttery blonde colour from his youth. He was a perpetrator of arcane systems, from the native quarter of some sunken, exotic city...

- Yawning lets the good energy out... - he'd tell students in his classes who were noticeably bored.

Dr Chopin surveyed a cadaver. The cadaver was some poor tortured soul with a face frozen in heartbreak, one Mike Ryko. Chopin got a pair of chest separators and parts the sternum.

- Look inside...

The class peered round in a circle into the bloody bunghole.

- We see the heart is stressed and hollow, like a burst balloon. The ventricles have ruptured and the entire atrium has gone a bruised blue colour…anyone care to offer a diagnostic?

- Broken heart sir, you can tell by the gradual decay in the bicuspid. There are some signs of hypoxemia, the heart looks choked of oxygen – suggested one student with scolded skin and a shaggy hair full of rats.

- Excellent. And do we know how he got here?

- His heart broke the moment he realised the familiar world around him was counterfeited.

- Good, and how do we know that?

- Distended jugular vein?

- Cardiogenic shock and apical ballooning in the takotsubo ventricle.

Chopin nodded with a pleased loom on his face.

- Yes, yes…anything else?

- Because he's black?

- NOOO! – Chopin cracked his cane over the idiot intern's skull.

- Not only does that make no sense, it violates the sense of etiquette any decent practitioner abides by. Realisation causes wraparound LAD, but look at his face. What's unique about his expression?

The interns studied the Ryko's agonised features closely.

- Anyone?

A series of blank faces stared back at him desperately.

- Neuralgia anyone? Realisation causes trigeminal neuralgia!

Most of the interns made an OOOOHHHH!!! Sound while a small group of the more serious students slapped their foreheads and cursed under their breath.

- Realisation of the Slave State causes the blood vessels in the face to inflate and press against the root nerve, obvious stuff class!

- There's also signs of a stress induced tumour, this is a sign that he might've been transmatic…
- one intern pointed to a bulge at Ryko's temple.

Chopin raised his cane above his head ready to thrash the little know-it-all sonofabitch.

SS

ELLIS HADN'T MASTURBATED ONCE SINCE he got to the Slave State. It previously bothered him that he hadn't been laid *at all* since arriving in San Francisco, now he felt like a neutered dog. The tightening colour around his neck was as castrating and emasculating as his chemical sterilisation…

From the ledge of a Shell County flop-house, he gazed out at the filthy, vanishing city and wondered what Sur was doing. Was he casually stalking his next hit? Or had it all gotten too much for him? Ellis imagined he might be writing songs on an acoustic guitar and taking part in peace rallies, the work of a hired killer didn't entirely suit Sur's image. He should have been lying on a tarp while naked hippie chicks braided his long tresses and fed him tokes from a ginormous spliff. Ellis hoped he was at least happy.

Everything in Shell seemed to emit plumes of vapour, of smog, the essence of life trying to escape through vents and pipes and the breath of fetid walking corpses. Ellis shared a room with a woman. He'd been there for over an hour before he decided to stop gazing forlornly out the window speaks to her. He asked her who she was and what her story was.

She said her name was Isabella. She was an actress. She was very beautiful.

- I came here with an old love of mine; or rather I was banished here alongside him.

Isabella explained that she'd fallen in love with a director and that they'd both initially been exiled to a place called the Zinc Theatre after his movie failed miserably at the box office. She tried explaining what the Zinc Theatre was but Ellis was too fried, too swollen with barely digestible new information that there simply wasn't room for any more – and that was fine, because meeting Isabella was the first positive thing that's happened since Ignius had been sucked into that trap with the silverfish.

- It was my own self-sabotage that saw me on that path to chaos. I remember a William Burroughs quote that reminds me of my own efforts of self-sabotage, "Every man (or in this case, woman) has inside them a parasitic being who is acting not at all to his (or her) advantage. Why do you spill things? Why do you drop something? You have the equipment there not to drop something. Why isn't that capacity used? Something is preventing it. And you come down t some sort of basic dualism. There isn't one person out there, but two. Acting against each other."

- You read that as if it were Shakespeare.

- It's better…

- What ever happened to you boyfriend the director?

- He lost control of the situation, as I knew he would in the end. He became a hopeless drug addict. We eventually made it out of the Zinc Theatre district. The director was murdered in cold blood by his producer and writer. I was almost molested and killed by his main actor in the movie, another troubled wad of protoplasm called Stanley. It was a terrible mess.

Isabella explained that the director had a drug habit that could not be quenched. Ellis had never been addicted to anything, he told her this (although he wasn't sure why), perhaps violence at one point in his life, but not now.

- Do you know someone called Mike Ryko? I was hoping to bump into him...

- I get the feeling that Mike Ryko was Transmatic?

- Well, no one is really 100% on that, but I believe he was.

- He was...

- Then you know him?

- All transmatic vessels are aware of those with the same gift.

- You're transmatic as well?

- I've always been aware of something, extrasensory within myself, but have a very muted version of it. Years of physical abuse and a familiarity with serfdom have dulled all my unique perceptions. I'm grateful for that. I'm still able to identify others of similar ability though...

- Do you know where Mike might be?

Isabella closed her eyes and shook her head sadly. Ellis knew what this meant.

- The truth Ignius, is that people who are transmatic can see through the fabric of the slave states parameters. This is a very dangerous and threatening gift to possess. Most people who do not collapse internally when they cross realms are lobotomised and killed. Mike never stood a chance.

- I see...

- I'm sorry. I get the feeling he was a significant person in the universe. His powers could have changed things for us, or at least led a successful uprising.

- I know he would've.

- Were you close?

- Not really, but in a way, he was the person closest to me. Well, Mike and Sur anyway. Do you miss the life outside this fucked up zone of hell?

- Honestly?

Ellis nodded.

- This place isn't any better than where I originally came from.

- Me either – agreed Ellis before adding – I can think of worse places to be...

NINE

UN SAT DOWN AT THE TRESTLE TABLE and shuffled his data papers. Moog wriggled into the high chair opposite, waiting. When he saw, his superior was comfortable and a suitable amount of time had passed, Un began to read.

– He's a Negro.

– Yes, and what else?

– He was born into serfdom, grew up in the pits. He also worked in a civil service job in Abbeville County, South Carolina, USA, a police sheriff.

– And he is settled?

– He's drugged up now. We won't know how distressed he's going to be when he regains lucidity, never mind have any indication if he'll willingly mate on request.

Orb scoffed indignantly at the notion.

– Well if he doesn't mate he'll be euthanized.

– Yes sir.

- Tell him this.

- Of course, sir.

- Anything else? No transferable venereal diseases I should know about? These insects scuttling around on Earth soil are notoriously afflicted when we bring them in for testing.

- No sir he's clean.

- Good.

- In fact, you might say we've done him a favour bringing him out of his own environmental context.

- How so?

- The white demographic has heavily chastised him. It's why he became a police officer, although he doesn't command the respect you might think.

- Well then, see if he's awake.

SS

UN PEERED THROUGH THE BAR-BEAMS of helium-neon. The naked specimen was curled up in a ball in the hay.

– Are you awake? – Un asked, quietly at first.

The Earthling stirred restlessly, then upon realising Un's presence outside his cell, scrambled to his feet.

– We have no intention of hurting you Negro…

– What did you just call me?

– Negro?

– You sonofabitch, what *are* you? What'd you want? – The Earthling's anger dissipated when he became aware of his nakedness. He clutched at his genitals, shielding them from view.

– We ask only one simple thing of you. Failure to comply with this request will result in extermination.

The Earthling's throat seized up.

– What do you want me to do?

- There is another human, a female in another cell – a Norwegian with pallid skin. You will mate with her.

The Earthling stood naked in quiescence, his face fast becoming contorted by inner conflict.

- I can't… - he eventually choked out.

- You *must*, or you'll be murdered.

- I…already have a partner…

Un stood a moment, scrutinising whether the human was being serious or indulging in sarcasm. When he saw the severity in his dark stare, Un knew him serious.

- *Monogamy?* Does such inclination still exist? You have stratospheric divorce rate on your planet. Unions which last are often sexless and absent of passion.

- Not always…

- Yes always! Here, on this planet, Ortega, we live in a much less sexually possessive culture and it has brought us nothing but happiness. Lifelong coupling is draconian, archaic, pointless. We live in egalitarian and peaceful groups and have consistently high rates of sexual interaction, as evidence of our natural inclinations, love without limits.

– No.

– Why do you glory in the ideal of monogamy, especially when your life is at risk?

– I *choose* to glory in monogamy.

– You are denying your own nature, I should know, I've spent my entire life studying and probing your species!

– Human brains are wired for social group interaction.

– And what of it?

– We crave the intimate synchrony of emotions. What do your people do for comfort and security?

The earthling looked at Un. He was a pink protoplasmic blob of tapioca pudding, an amoeba with advanced sentience, and now he looked stumped.

- Listen Negro, the female awaits you. She is comely, do not refuse…

- You don't understand. I *can't* mate with a woman.

- And why not?

- Because…that *would* be against my nature. The Slave state hasn't distorted who I really am.

Un motioned backwards in horror.

- A homosexual? – The alien blob uttered, accusingly. The Earthling did not respond, only sat back down in a hill of hay.

- On this planet, homosexuality is as detrimental to our existence as a nuclear holocaust.

- You'd think that were the case on Earth also…

- Any variation on the sexual function which deviates from procreation is flawed. You must mate with the girl!

- Why do *I* have to do it?

- Because, despite what you may think, we are not trying to hurt you, we are trying to save you!

<u>SS</u>

UN LOOKED AT THE NUDE HUMAN. His skin was iridescent under the gaze of Ortega's twin moonlets.

What a waste – Un thought, *for this specimen to shun his calling. He would make many beautiful, intellectually gifted offspring, enough to save and re-populate the desolate ruins of Earth. Perhaps were he made aware of the situation, he might be more willing to cooperate.*

Un gulped and his transparent membrane changed colour with shame.

- Your planet has been destroyed by radon gases.

- What?

- These gases came from our planet. Following our attempts to mitigate the harmful chemicals radiating from our mine enclaves, we unintentionally deflected a large portion into your planet's atmosphere. It was an accident.

- You bastards...

Un became a wobbling canvas of guilt.

- We are seeking to remedy our error. At Ortega, we have sought permission from the Galactic Council to spearhead Earth reparation. The Slave State is run by us now. Our planet has been so ensconced by Earth's demise and its consequences that we have dedicated our lives to helping mend the mistake we created. We are taking responsibility.

The Earthling felt tightness in his chest. He thought about his partner and the crushing comprehension that he had been, by the law of averages, decimated by the radioactive onslaught along with the majority.

– We were *all* killed?

– There were others on Earth, a clutch of survivors dotted throughout the continents, but the pollutants have left all but two men completely infertile. You are one of those men. You see now that you must do as we say.

– Use the other guy.

– He is currently in stasis. His genes are weak, his intelligence low. Dan Smear is not someone we want to resort to. Using subjective measures and circular reasoning one might deduce that your homosexuality merely veils your latent heterosexuality. Your negative experiences with women have manifested…

– Let me stop you there, I have had a wonderful relationship with women.

- Do you want your species to die forever?

Un became angry by what he perceived as irrational intractability.

- Better your species die than you insert your seamen into a female?

The Earthling considered this; his sexuality did not define him. This was surely a matter which transcended both his pride and sense of self, therefor it was passable that he put such facets of himself to the darkest crook of his mind, if only for that singular act. The Earthling felt himself about to agree to the Ortega people's demands.

SS

HE WAS LED AT GUNPOINT to the cell containing the Norwegian woman. He caught a glimpse of her on his way in; even he could not deny her intrinsic beauty. They would indeed make attractive children. A gelatinous Ortegian guard pushed a button on a control panel and the bar-beams ceased to imprison. The man was nudged forward, lunging forth in the girl's direction. He landed on his knees. She smiled faintly, sensing something reluctant about the man chosen to impregnate her. The guard backed away from the Earth creatures and hit the switch to bring the bars up once again.

– I am Asta – said the girl in broken English.

– I'm Samuel.

The girl glanced at Samuel's breechcloth. She was evidently attracted to him and could not contain her delight that he had been selected. *Asta loved black men.* Noticing the joy and excitement dancing across her face, Samuel leaned in as if to whisper, cupping his hand over the girl's ear before revealing – I must confess something to you Asta. I have never been attracted to a woman, not since my own mother. This is going to be difficult for me. Asta's face was a portrait of disappointment and betrayal. She jerked away from Samuel. The Ortegians started to murmur in discontent.

– *Has she rejected the male?*

– *Because he is black in the skin?*

- No, she told us she likes them that colour!

- Then what's the problem?

Un stood nervously, watching the awful scene unfold. He had to do *something*. Desperately clambering to the podium above the herd of miners, Un coughed into a mic to get everyone's attention.

- Ok everyone, let's give these two some privacy. We need controlled circumstances. Even humans don't fuck in front of a crowd you know. Let's move it along!

SS

UN COULD TELL THAT ASTA was furious to the point of violence. She had already torn free her brassiere and breechcloth and was advancing on the male. Samuel was cowering in the corner of the cell, the burning neon beams inches from the bare flesh of his back. She had her hands around his throat, squeezing with the superhuman strength of emotional rejection. Samuel grabbed the girl by the wrist, managed to shift her power. The girl went careening across the cell into a hay stack. Asta lay motionless in the wet dirt. Samuel looked out at the alien race looking in. He caught the stare of Un who suddenly filled up with piercing guilt, not for the first time.

SS

MOOG APPEARED BESIDE UN ON the podium.

- What do you think the Earthlings would do if they realised they are our creators?

Un kept his stare locked on the male Earthling in the cage.

- I imagine their heads would explode.

Moog gave a hideous cackle then abruptly stopped when he noticed the despair in Un's countenance.

- Why are you so upset? The Galactic Council have been very understanding about our predicament, you know that. They don't hold anything against us. We tried our best, they will not punish us greatly for this failure.

- There is always sadness when one supersedes their own God, especially in the cruel way we went about achieving superiority.

- The Radon was an accident!

- Was it?

Moog ignored the moroseness of his secretary and addressed the miners who were both confused and disturbed by the events.

- It seems, good Ortegians that God is dead. Let us mourn.

TEN

FOR A WHILE THERE WAS SILENCE...

- It zigzags, watch...

Ellis lit the fuse and took a leap back. The rocket sent a spiral arm into the starless sky. When it reached a certain point in the atmosphere it exploded, dispersing fiery shards of light over the valley.

– Neat – decided Isabella.

– I was thinking of using them for the Slave State Festival tomorrow.

Ellis was desperate to impress her. She was kind, beautiful, talented and scarred through to her very soul – he'd never met anyone quite like her. Of course, there were other benefits to dating Isabella. She was an actress and therefor immune to Slave State conscription.

– D'you know any neat tricks? I know a few card tricks.

She thought for a moment.

 – When I was 16 I first learned how to pull off the curse of the blinding worm.

– What's that? – Ellis sat up eagerly. Isabella started reciting.

> *– Needle in thread*
> *Needle in bread*
> *Eye in needle*
> *Needle in eye*

Bury the bread deep in a sty

Ellis tried not to laugh in Isabella's face.

- You don't believe I can do it, do you?

- I do, really, I do!

- You'd take a clump of mouldy bread, run a needle through it and bury the bread under the fence of a pigsty. If you chanted the spell properly the worm materialised behind the accursed's eyeball, blinding them instantly – curse of the blinding worm.

- That *is* neat...

- My mother taught many of today's leading sorcerers the ways of malevolent magical practice, from Himmlue to Zazapeechwa. In Virginia, the underground war was fought almost entirely with necromancy. I'm not a part of that world anymore, don't worry.

- You became an actress?

- I *became* a ghost.

No one fell in love anymore, if the Slave State mottoes were to be believed anyway.

True love is dead and YOU have killed him!

…. for the longest time, Ellis sincerely believed that. This was just the way of it – except he *had* fallen in love, intensely in love, with Isabella. They sat until the night started to show glimmers of sun-up. Ellis collected his novelty fireworks and walked Isabella back into Shell County. The scorched star pushed through, the ground would soon be blistered by it.

SS

THE HOWLS OF AGONY CAME and didn't stop, like a wolf baying at the moon. The first days of the festival had begun. Shell County had loin-cloth clad slaves by the hundred. Men were chained together, forced to march down the street while being whipped by their slave-master. He worked them like devils, especially in preparation for the festival. Ellis watched on, counting his blessings. He couldn't handle life in the mining enclaves. He wasn't made of strong enough stuff.

The master's whip was a substitute for food – it never lost its virtue. Some of the men were covered in sores from dragging the shafts of the rickshaw all day long. They could moan in discomfort, but nothing too theatrical or disruptive. Most had been enslaved so long they had come to believe they needed the State. If they returned to free, civilised society they wouldn't be able to cope. Of course, the best jobs for a slave involved working for officials rolling pats of butter, boiling Baroness Un's eggs, pounding ice or grinding coffee. However, the majority found themselves down the mine shafts.

SS

ISABELLA MADE HER WAY THROUGH the marching band of captives.   They barely registered her presence. Ellis watched Isabella disappear into the crush of ogling spectators, unable to know for sure if he'd ever see her again.

Pig-faced children scuffled hard in the silvery streets, troughs piling high, awful slander spoken in barbed oinking. Trash cans overflow/Wednesday summer heat send lines of reeking flesh up into the swirling vortex-hole where the sun used to be before it fell out of the sky and into the ocean. Women wept the eternal ballad, histrionic moans - sounds of nightmare trains rumbling on the distant track of thinking...

SS

SCIENTOLOGIST PROMISES. A TROUPE OF youths carrying their slave master atop his throne down the tormented street to pigs puffing pan-pipe soundtrack...

One of the boys, dark hair, simple doughy features, says to his friend, blonde and tall, ill-looking.

- The master has put on weight.

The tall blonde nauseous kid shushes, sends spit all over his raised, erect index. He's scared the master will hear.

- He can't hear us – reassures the dark-haired kid – he's too wrapped up in all the attention.

SS

ELLIS JOINED THE ONLOOKERS, SOME of whom had taken to hurling rotten fruit at the children. He saw a child, the dark-haired boy, and recognised him. A distant familiarity: *a son-a brother-a cousin-another?* He thought about the worm wriggling behind the milky cornea. It was the recent, profound rumblings of love knotting his gut into a vice-tight noose that made him think clearly about the slave-children. Instead of simple gratitude (that he had avoided the shackles of slavery himself), Ellis felt something real for the boy, an emotion humanity almost forgot. Then Ellis remembered that "True love was dead" and HE had killed him....

He went to the store to buy some more novelty fireworks.

For a while more there would be silence…

PART THREE

ELEVEN

Ellis

FOLLOW THE SOUND OF GRINDING MOLARS AND MOANING DRUGGIES....

....an Italian straight off the sidewalk, a professional gambler (most likely) with a big thuggish outward show came into the apartment, brought out a clear bag with some of his own private *stuff* from his back pocket and sat cross-legged in the circle of other junkies. He put some in a tablespoon, tamped it with a wet finger-tip and held it over a flame until it bubbled and cracked. Ignius Ellis sat right across from the thuggish Italian. He was a curious looking junkie, noted Ellis, strong shouldered with good skin and oily hair. There was a macho bulge in the crotch of his faded jeans that was the antithesis of a drained and sex-starved addict. Mysterious eyes rebounded off each face in the circle. He didn't reveal his name until prompted 20 minutes into the communal experience.

– Gio – he said softly, dreamily.

Ignius's first impression was that he might be good to score from. Gio had the look of a man people rarely fucked with. He was struck by how healthy the big Italian seemed.

– What's yer secret pal?

– Huh? What?

– You cooking sleeping tablets over there?

– Nah man, this is my own shit.

Ignius's feeling about Gio suddenly changed. It was apparent upon closer scrutiny that a soul radiated healthily from his young face. There was *no way* he was a Jammer.

- Can we try some? It's all about sharing in this joint...

Gio gave an uncertain look. Ellis gave a laugh and told him to relax.

- I wouldn't take your shit mate, I'm just kiddin' on. It'd be insane to expect a Jammer like yourself to share his own personal stash. Say, you're a right handsome fella.

- Why you sassin' me?

- Am I sassing you?

- You keep lookin at me funny, what's the matter?

- I'm just lookin mate...

- Well why you lookin all untrusting?

- Because the druggies in this building are brothers and sisters, one big family. We respond only to the overtures of our fellow addicts, not a filthy informant...

- Hey man, I ain't no narc!

Ellis rolled up his shirt sleeve and Gio initially thought he was about engage him in a fist-fight, but Ignius just pricked himself with a 30-gauge spike and exhaled.

- I beg to differ. Now don't worry. I'm a fair man, in fact we're all fair people here. It's a frequent misconception that all Jammers are hostile and self-serving. We're very amiable, made that way in no small part to the Jam-Caps themselves. Here's how it'll go...

The Italian's petulance was revealing. Jammers weren't paranoid or indignant. Gio's arms shot around all over the place.

- Hey man, fuck you ok, I can stay and shoot up if I want. I got let in at the door, I got my own shit and just wanna hit off the streets...

Ellis shared a glance with the other junkies in the user's circle.

- Did you know I've killed men before, hmm, did you know that Gio?

- Yeah? Big woop! – The Italian put on his best snot-nosed face.

- Most of the people in this circle have killed men before. The Jam-Caps keep us nice and affable, but you know the tendency for old habits to creep back up on a man?

- Oh yeah, who you killed?

- Before I came to the State I was a hitman, before that I was a hooligan back home in Scotland.

- Yeah?

- The man next to you has killed before, haven't you Roy?

A stick-insect man with long braided hair and a baggy blue shirt open at his chest jutted to attention. He had an eye missing.

- Sure, I mean, I killed a girl once. I shot her in the back of the head. It wasn't nothin personal. I just wanted to try it out, yano? Felt good, no Jam-Cap high but I could kill again for a kick.
Gio stood up, his mask of coolness slipping right away to reveal a scared kid. Ellis stood up and faced him.

- You're out yer depth big man. Take your sleepin' pills and tell the State to go fuck their ugly, extra-terrestrial mothers. Now scram...

<u>*SS*</u>

Despite the warmth of the jungle, there was such a prominent coldness in the ditch of Ignius Ellis's soul that it made his breath freeze into a solid funnel of ice. The tumult of river and rocks in perpetual conflict were all around him. Blood coursed through his skull in chorus with the rapids. A mirror image of Ignius came out from the thickets - a version free of the awful knowledge of the Slave State. He was afraid to go near it for fear of corrupting it somehow, as if the truth were contagious and deadly to peaceful, ignorant animals.

Staring

Staring back

The crashing elementals in his ears spiral duct. Then the smells - a floppy slab of flesh skewered and rotating above the glowing coals of a fire. He reached out with his hand to touch himself and felt the chisel-cold skin. His mirror image went to the river's edge and waded his bare feet in the surge of brawling water.

He woke up in a bed in a strange room. He didn't know if he was still in the jungle or if it'd all been a dream and he was back in his own, much more familiar, urban nightmare.

The pleasant warmth of black coffee on the inside of his throat and its bitter aftertaste on his tongue

His temples throbbed.

– Don't let anyone tell you what to do, ye hear me? – Ignius' father said in a serious tone, telling his son what to do. Ignius listened and nodded to confirm that he wouldn't do what anyone told him – except his father, of course!

– I want to punch you in the personality… – he mumbled to himself, thinking of his father.

Ellis pushed his fingers into his eyes to nurse the headache somehow, the veins on the inside of his lids lit up like fractures of lightening.

In hell, they cover your head over

So, you can't see what's going on

As if they want to hide the atrocities of the burning metropolis

So, they can really relish the expression on your face upon the big unveiling

You're bundled into the back of a vehicle

It takes off at breakneck speed and all you can hear is the skidding and the clumsy shifting of gears

And all you can see is life inside a paper bag.

THE END

Excerpt from _MURDERLAND by Garrett Cook_ from MorbidbookS. Read Like The Devil.

Book 1: H8

"There's a brand new dance, but I don't know its name
That people from bad homes do again and again
It's big and it's bland full of tension and fear
They do it over there, but they don't do it here."

-David Bowie- *"Fashion"*

What a Wonderful World

I.

Sometimes he has the courtesy to wear shades. There is something oh-so-thrilling about making the asshole behind the desk feel like losing his lunch, but this time he doesn't. This time, he is wearing the shades, but it isn't quite courtesy, no, he doesn't really know the meaning of the word. He does this so the man will be able to look at him, and he'll be able to look down over them and cause drama, cause the man's blood to turn to ice. He waits for the question that bothers him most to do it.

"So, Jack, what made you want to do what you do now?"

He waits for it. He's been working on his timing for awhile. 3, 2, 1…0. He always includes the zero when he counts down, and that's when he goes. Down come the shades, and the surgically enlarged mandibles expand into a smile that other mouths are incapable of.

"Well, Richard, all the cowboy and astronaut slots were filled up."

He smiles, although he stares through time, looking through the crack in the closet door to see a room full of old boxes, neglected tools and dusty books. The place where they put the forgotten things. He hears the squeal of joy in the distance, knowing his mother is lifting it into the air or tickling it. He hears the front door open and the heavy footsteps of his stepfather. Only a few hours until everybody goes to bed and his mother brings up a little tray of food. Why live when you don't exist? He watches himself close his eyes and pretend that nothing is there, but he knows when he opens them the closet and the family and the baby will be there. If he closed his eyes on the set, the talk show would still be there, the audience would still be there, the Sun, big burning zero betrays its nature. We can only do what we can. There is less and less every day, someday, some wonderful day...

II.

The pimp likes the prophet, but the prophet is never sure about the pimp. The prophet opens the box, and the pimp smiles. He genuinely wants to hug the old man, although the stench is nigh unbearable. The pimp claps his hands, and the girl brings a stack of papers. The prophet looks them over, reads words that nobody else knows are there and nods his approval.

"Will this help?" asks the pimp, who genuinely wonders, although the old man's box is worth several hundred dollars.

"We can only do what we can," says the prophet. He knows hundreds of others think the same thing.

114

III.

Stupid fucking clowns. King shit Kyle springs his swordcane and Joey can't help but sigh. Joey draws his knife and tries to let them know he means business with his eyes. The Gacys aren't armed. Who would have expected them to be. They're big, but they're not armed. Their leader looks his boys over and looks Kyle's boys over and knows sure as mama's monthlies they're dusties if they even bother. Joey knows that Kyle just wants to make a mess though, if he wants to pomp he should go ahead and pomp, find some sweet bait make meatloaf. The top hat falls over Kyle's eyes as he advances.

Joey can't help but laugh. *Mr. Badass Ripkid leader made-up as the scourge of Whitechapel thinks he can stack the dusties but he can't even wear his fuckin' hat right. It seems for a second like a stupid way of life, but how else are you gonna feel free? So fuck 'im. Go along with it. Swallow your pride. Kyle's pathetic, but we can only do what we can.*

A Walk in the Park

The grey-haired man I've been following looks down at his watch yet again and yet again starts to fidget a little. He knows that the woman starts jogging at 8 pm every night. 5'2, blonde, 24, it could be said nubile as all fuck. The mundanes are over there chatting away about what Ashley said to Chris and then how Chris was out with Julie at the Johnny Rockets at the mall when he told Ashley he had to stay home and watch his little cousin. What scandal. I hope they set that bastard straight. Chatting away with a mechanical whir. Fucking robots. Cut them open and see all the wires for myself. See the electric guts and polymer skin. See the silicon brains. But I get back to ignoring them because I don't like the noises they make. Every night without fail when she goes jogging, the grey-haired man is there. I have not checked every night, but on my way home from work, I have checked frequently enough to know that every night without fail he is there. He's neither fat nor jolly, but the media has dubbed him Kris Kringle. This is because he is known to leave brightly wrapped packages full of their organs on the doorsteps of their families like a proud kitty cat. Or like Santa Claus, as they think of it.

Kris is the grownup equivalent of the precocious child who takes apart daddy's watch to see how it works. He deconstructs things. Returns them to where they came from when he's done. A savage who thinks he's a scientist. I don't know his story, but I know his work. I have, as I mentioned, been watching him. I've sat in the park at 8 o'clock too watching the young blond filthy yellow cunt filthy filthy filthy yellow cunt little mommy fills it up dumps it out, full then dropped off, full then empty, squeezes me out and doesn't think my little eyes might have looked and seen and remembered the bright gold sheen like all the other blondes not about that. Not about grudges. Fast, anonymous, above such things. Calm down and do it. Get home and document it, write it down, write it down, keep it near your head always keep it near your head. This is not for anyone to see. This is for me. This is not exhibit B or the documentary, this is for me. I am fast, I am anonymous; it is a matter of principle.

But I wonder what this guy's doing tonight. What card from the less than full deck he's working with does he want to play? What the fuck is his angle? Bag of groceries. Fuck you, Kringle. It's not that I doubt it will work, I know it's about 95% likely to, but it's sad and banal. It shows no respect for her intelligence. Simple trap. Animalistic. Primitive like him. Bag of groceries, my ass. I would like to think that she'd be smarter, but no. And I'd like to think that I could leave her to him. She'd be dead anyway, no real chance of bearing the child, but no, I can't let it happen. I have to do this. If he does it, she's just another thing to be taken apart, if I do it, then she dies for a reason, which is I think the least a woman dead at 24 could ask for. I'll just walk up, turn on my winning smile, lure her somewhere and open up the briefcase. She deserves better than this loser. I will smile, flash my big brown eyes, give her what she does deserve and GET THE FUCK HOME.

I hate this part of it, I honestly do. I just want to kill the little yellow sluts before the Dark Ones start to fill them up with their seeds and then they make more like me. Like what I should have been. They thought they had created the perfect little general for their legions. Charming, handsome, nice eyes, toned body, IQ 236. Gacy and Berkowitz combined. And most likely an average human being ahead of Mr. Kringle. And unlike the previously mentioned two, I am not gay, I am not stupid and I DON'T want to get caught. I am a righteous avenger of the wrongs done by my creators. I am retribution turned against monsters who make me do this. Who build the robots and the robots just walk around with their slow computer brains and wire guts and every once in awhile it seems there is a glitch in the program and the robots start to tear and dismantle each other. Mostly, there are robots mostly. But I look at the jogger, and I know that that little yellow cunt is made of skin and organs and juices and is ready, more than ready, ready and willing to be filled up with corruption by the Dark Ones in order to make another devil, another one of me, to come and to undo all my good works and all of my crusading and everything that makes me me and carry my head on a prideful pike and I can't FUCKING STAND IT. They will not duplicate me. I will destroy the devil factories the clone machines DEEP BREATH don't fuck up I won't fuck up I won't I won't I won't. Stand up, be casual. Look like a robot, look like a person. Don't look like anything special. Subtle, discreet, nondescript, Mr. Casual, Mr. Suave.

And then there's Kringle, suspicious, scary, more than a little off. Nothing avuncular, pleasant or especially trustworthy about him. He stands up, limping a little, plays up his age more than enough. That should have been enough for her to realize something's up. I have to wonder if she watches the news, if she sees the T-shirts and the DVDs and the television shows and the baseball caps, videogames, and the newspaper. He asks if she can help him with his groceries, help load them in his car, says he's got a bad back and hunches over to emphasize it. Then how did he carry them three blocks from the grocery store to his car, parked suspiciously in an alley near a public park? Why did he not park outside of the grocery store to begin with instead of a dark alley near a public park? It might be a public park in the Safe Zone, but still too many questions. I shudder when I once more realize that he'll still get away with it.

Too many questions. But, she doesn't ask any of them. Walks with him to the alley. Quick strike with a blunt object, dragged into the back seat. I do have to hand it to him, he's pretty strong and pretty good at parking discreetly. I take note of the license plate and the next day; call my friend Shauna at the DMV. As Godless

Jack Cavanagh wrote in "The Complete Reaper," a photographic memory is one of a psychopomp's handiest tools. I find the car is registered to a Joe Strickland. Strickland. Eww. He'll never be too famous with a name like that. Nothing sinister. Nothing especially melodic or intense about it.

Joe Strickland, alias Kris Kringle. Alias Karl Edward Pratt. I see the name on the paper on his front lawn. Karl Edward Pratt. There we go. Much better reaper name than Strickland. Definitely. Kill count 14. Nowadays 14 makes it a hobby. Not a star, never. A murder enthusiast. I come to his house with my silenced .22 in my pocket. I hate guns, but I want this to end fast. This will be the first man I have ever killed and I would rather it be the last. I want this C list poseur barbarian out of my way and out of my mind once and for all.

I ring his doorbell. He comes to the door in a bathrobe. Part of me hates the idea of shooting a guy in a bathrobe. It seems like such an embarrassing way for someone to die. But then again, to be killed by this loser, whose handle has been mentioned on the news a mere three times. He's 55, 56 maybe. Way too old. He's in a young man's game, too. His face is sunken and tired, his teeth tobacco stained. His gnarled, craggy hands light a cigarette out of a three-dollar pack.

"Something I can do you for you, young man?"

"Kris Kringle? Kill count 14?"

A smile crosses his face. It's always flattering to these guys when some armchair detective tracks them down for an autograph or a picture together or to answer some questions for his website. He probably hasn't had any yet. Godless Jack's address is on his website. There have been 28 published interviews with the I-80 Roadflare Stalker I've been told, 17 with the Ice Cream Truck Strangler. But not much Kris Kringle material, no. Derisive, stupid, primitive. Gimmicky, they think. I feel a little sick being mistaken for a fan of a pathetic son of a bitch like Karl Edward Pratt. A fan. I shudder to think how desperate, depraved and stupid his fans must be.

"No," I answer, my face grim and stony, "a fellow psychopomp."

He goes through newspaper clippings in his head. Thinks about Oscar coverage. Thinks about BLD news. Then moves on to the local Bundys. It's clear he is doing this because he examines my profile, the contours of my face, tries to get to the bottom of it. He doesn't recognize me. Of course he doesn't. I'm not a celebrity. I'm not a role model. I have no merchandise and my killings can't be rented at the local Blockbuster, so of course, he doesn't know my face. I relish it.

"Jeremy Jenkins."

Once more, he searches for the name and struggles idly for my face.

"What's your handle?"

I huff. "I don't have one."

Why does nobody see that I'm up to something more important? No end of annoyance. No fucking end of annoyance. My dissatisfaction registers heavily and he thinks I'm offended for an entirely different reason. Then again, who wouldn't?

"Don't worry, kid. You keep it up and maybe someday…"

"I haven't been caught."

He still doesn't get it. Very slow on the uptake.

"You should do something about that. Try letters. You really oughta read Godless Jack's books. They've done wonders for me."

I huff once again. "I don't need advice. The blonde in the park was mine."

The skinny grey old bag puts out his cigarette. "Look kid, I'm just doin' my best to get by. I'm trying to get some attention, some coverage. I can't go round worryin' who belongs to whom. It ain't my problem if some 'pomp can't stack the dusties. My meat's my meat; your meat's yours, man. You do your shit and you're still choked to death, ain't my problem. When the bait's sweet, it's sweet."

"You're nothing."

These are the last words he ever hears. I shoot him. He's nobody.

Television Man is Crazy

"In Ohio and Indiana, authorities report that Bundy award nominee, the I-80 Roadflare Stalker struck again. At 46 kills, it's possible he might just bring home the Bundy. What do you think Valerie?"

"Well, Chet, The Roadflare is definitely a contender this year and since Jack Cavanagh voluntarily removed himself from the Bundy runnings, it seems that Mr. Right, the I-80 Roadflare and Hacksaw Sally…"

"Nice to see a lady in the runnings, isn't it, Valerie?"

"Oh, definitely, Chet, if you ask me it's high time…"

The remote clicks. The talking heads bantering sport talk fade into cathode hell, burning and writhing alongside frames too numerous to mention. Cass yawns her way up from the quilt, and stretches up as if grabbing for something on the ceiling. The falling quilt reveals round breasts the color of bread dough and sharp russet nipples. Jeremy feels like rolling over and touching them, pinching them, kissing them, biting them, suckling on them just a bit, but Jeremy is trying to decide whether he believes she is a robot or not. He's seen inside her, tasted her and it feels warm enough in there. Oh, God, it feels warmer than anywhere to Jeremy. But, it might just be some kind of plastics from the dimension the Dark Ones come from. After all, she, like all the others watches all the murders on the TV going down, places bets on her favorites, screams in the chatrooms now and again, jeers the boring ones and maintains the brand loyalty that only a true junkie can have. She is entertained. In the middle of all of the shit and the violence and the noise and the death, she is entertained. Sometimes she might be entertained by the irony, sometimes by the repugnant nature of what this country has become. Sometimes by the chittering stupidity of the inane newscasters and the cacophonous blaring of the loud and pointless commercials. She is occasionally disgusted by how far this has gone. By how reap culture has been perverted from its purer forms and reduced to a pop culture cult.

It used to be just people who really understood why people kill and the defiance and the intensity involved. It didn't used to be stupid teenagers who didn't even know the names Jack the Ripper or Albert de Salvo, although there are still plenty who idolize those two.

But still, so often she can't tear herself away from it. It makes Jeremy debate whether she is in fact one of the few intelligent people he has ever met, or if she is falling for the game too, just falling into the pit they dig for people who are looking too close. He stops and thinks about the razors he keeps in the briefcase and about how there might just be wires in her, God don't let there be wires, he thinks, god don't let there be wires. Don't let there be the fiberoptic cables that link up to the receivers for satellite images. Don't let there be neural uplinks to the Dark Ones. His breathing gets heavy and there begins to be a burning feeling in his eyes. His head begins to throb violently with a humming like a fork against a violin string. He cannot stop thinking about wires and cables and the mechanical whirring of the machines around him. Cass leans over and kisses him and relief washes over Jeremy's feverish brain. Human. Of course. Should have known. She is, after all a brunette. The Dark Ones will never touch her.

"I love you," she says. Her face gets bright and she looks at him as if he was the most interesting thing she had ever seen. She looks at him like a sunset.

"I love you," he replies.

And it is all that he feels. All he wants to say and know and think about. He returns her kiss voraciously. It expands and moves around her mouth. The kiss, once small has become a colossus. They roll over on top of each other. They writhe and shake, they coil around one another and they begin to explode with power and intensity. Jeremy's eyes are full of astronomy. The movements of planets and the blazing of bright new stars shine in them. His perpetual motion superpowered Swiss watch brain lets itself shut off, lets itself return to its roots as meat and juices. Cass sort of sees somebody she was a few thousand years back in Egypt or Mesopotamia or somewhere of the sort. She remembers being as she is at the moment: naked and exalting in the triumph of being and the movements of everything. There is Jeremy and there is Cass and they are creation. Crashing like waves and falling like torrents of rain.

And then Jeremy's elbow hits the remote and the channel changes. The room fills with venom oozing from the television and Jeremy can feel it. Jeremy smells the cloud of noxious hate and feels the flames of persecution lick at his feet. He feels more than a little sick.

"Karl Edward Pratt, Kris Kringle, was found dead in his home today at the age of 57. Kringle was killed by a shot to the head from a .22 revolver. Kringle was known for the particularly inventive and grisly qualities of his murders, involving dismembering his victims and delivering body parts to their families. His killings numbered 14 to date. And while compared to others, that might seem to be few, he will still be remembered for the viciously ingenious nature of those he committed. Pratt's identity was discovered only when police found a kitchen full of human parts and wrapping paper. The media and the American people alike remained ignorant of the identity of the visionary that so ably captured their attention. Karl Edward Pratt you will be missed. This is a true American tragedy."

124

The newsanchor, no longer a portrait of stony, ersatz integrity looks genuinely dismayed. He purses his lip in dissatisfaction in one of those rare moments during which he finds something truly sad. Jeremy is not altogether certain that those moments exist and is skeptical that somebody like Pratt would have earned one. But, this is the typical death knell of a minor celebrity. Thorough appreciation, a tragedy painted so eloquently, a career exaggerated. An explosion of relevance onto the life and the TV screen alike. Then, suddenly, the tragedy fades from the news anchor's face. The relevance oozes down a drain behind his desk. He straightens up, perks up and turns to the woman at the desk beside him, the bleach blond with the low-cut blouse and the wrong shade of lipstick. Jeremy wonders if she's related to the identical news anchor on channel 8.

"Back to you, Eileen."

Cass finally shuts off the TV and a frown spreads across her face.

"That's too bad," she says, "I kinda liked his work. And it's occasionally nice to see them cover something besides Godless Jack or Hacksaw Sally. And sometimes, he was just amazing. He really had his moments. Like when he sent the Haskell girl's parents her stomach and it was full of his cum, I mean, Jesus," her tone changes. It's more upbeat, more excited.

"And the statement her folks gave the press was completely priceless, totally vintage," Cass launches into a bad Texas drawl, "we appeal to you, our fellow Americans, to help get Safe Zone regulations repealed and get monsters like the so-called Kris Kringle who did this to our daughter off the streets. Gina was the most precious gift that God ever gave us and while we cannot have her back, new laws will allow many many people to have their little girls come back home."

Cass falls into utter paroxysms of laughter and Jeremy heaves a very long sigh. He looks angry.

"Cass, they're human beings and they lost their daughter. It's not funny. Imagine how your parents would feel. What would they be saying on their news if they lost you to some maniac? What would I be saying?"

Disgust creeps into Cass. She'll never get used to his moments of moralizing. They come so briefly and they seem so goddamn random.

"Maniac? Maniac? You're so backward sometimes, Jeremy, you know that? I can't believe you're using that word. Catholic school really must have gotten to you. Maniac. God, these people have problems, Jeremy. Real honest to God psychological problems. But they overcome adversity and rise up to provide us with hours of quality entertainment every week. Talk like that makes you no better than guys like Tommy Simmons and the Christian Victim's front. You should go out and...and..."

Jeremy has heard this from Cass as much as Cass has heard Jeremy's tirades. Just as much as she didn't want him to open his mouth about it, he does not want to hear it from her. So, Jeremy does the one thing that any right-thinking red-blooded American male does in such a circumstance: he acquiesces.

"I'm sorry, Cass, you're right. I was just saying that it was in kind of poor taste, because, well, you know, they have a right to be angry. After all, they did lose someone they love to this person. They might not have a right to scorn or be bigoted or persecute, since society has progressed beyond punishing people for being who they are, you're right. But, by the same token, you can't really blame the victims; they're people too, aren't they?"

Much of the time Jeremy does not quite believe this. In fact, much of the time, Jeremy does not believe this at all, as in this day and age, real human beings seem to Jeremy to be few and far between. And it is hard to fully process a concern for the rights of victims when one is in fact killing them. Jeremy is taking note of this, but still tires of such behavior in others.

"Sometimes, Jeremy, you're just too nice. It's a mean world."

She kisses him once more and it is a little less so.

He grumbles angrily in his mind at how they could possibly devote a whole news report to sheer trash like Pratt. No real reputation, no ideas that could benefit a community, no real redeeming social graces and even as a source of entertainment, he could often be pretty mediocre. TV is really puzzling to Jeremy, sometimes. As Jeremy often does, he wonders exactly what it is that makes him not a monster. This is more of a logical exercise than a line of deep moral questioning. In fact, he very quickly comes up with a variety of highly satisfying replies to this question. He remembers, first of all, that he is above guilt. It is something to be banished from his mind. He is above guilt and beyond evil actions. Jeremy Jenkins, it turns out, is far too relevant to deal in murky moral absolutes. Jeremy does the right thing. He stops and savors the quiet produced by all the squealing, mewling, nasty little Dark Ones that he has kept from emerging and kept from spreading the seeds of ignorance and wrath. Only this and Cass bring him the requisite peace and time to clear this head and allow him to enjoy the knowledge that thanks to Jeremy Jenkins, Paladin and Patriot the world is safe. He smiles down on Cass and means it. So seldom does he mean it. So often is the smile a tool and a sidearm. Cass has fallen asleep which is a shame because he considers letting her know that were he to divulge his actions he would be a media sensation, and that whether he does or not, he is a rebel genius and the greatest killer since the Black Death. He is not often proud of it, but she might very well be. He thinks about just how adoring and fawning she would be if she knew about his work, but realizes that he needs to remain anonymous. That TV and such things don't really become him much. He considers slicing her open and checking for wires, but instead he delicately and subtly lets his fingers slip into her, feels the chills and excitement of her not seeing or knowing about all kinds of manipulations and maneuvers.

No, no TV for him.

"I'm not a superstar," he tells himself, "I'm a superman."

End excerpt …

'click' on hyperlink to get Kindle copy of
MURDERLAND from MorbidbookS.

ABOUT CHRIS KELSO

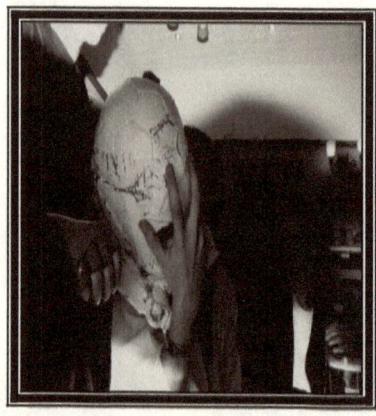

Chris Kelso is a writer, illustrator, editor, librarian and journalist from Scotland. Along with Garret Cook he is the co-creator/editor of anti-New Yorker zine "Imperial Youth Review".

He has yet to make any actual money from his shitty books....

Other works also by the author –

Novellas

A Message from the Slave State

Moosejaw Frontier

Transmatic

Short-story collections

Schadenfreude

Novels

The Dissolving Zinc Theatre

The Black Dog Eats the City

Magazines (Garrett Cook)

Imperial Youth Review issue 1

Imperial Youth Review issue 2

Comics

The New Animal Liberation Front

Anthologies

Caledonia Dreamin' – Strange Fiction of Scottish Descent (ed. With Hal Duncan)

Terror Scribes (ed. With Adam

HERE'S A LITTLE BITTY-BIT ABOUT THE HOUSE:

Where rules no longer apply. Where profane things occur. What hellions read. So, treat your dark self to our insane horror and edgy thrillers. The brutal bible tales. Explore our dark suspense and depraved monsters. Places far off the reservation. The strangest and most entertaining stories anywhere …

Go to MorbidbookS. Where everything bleeds. All MorbidbookS titles are available in paperback and kindle-style e-books at amazon.com, createspace.com and barns&noble.com and discerning serial killers near you.

ALSO AVAILABLE FROM Morbidbook S IN PRINT & KINDLE:

(click on any image in this book for hyperlink ...)